A Girl With A Cape™

and her jar of pennies

Written by Amy Logan

Illustrated by Rich Green

Published by Full Heart Publishing

A Girl With A Cape

and her jar of pennies

Written by
Amy Logan

Illustrated by
Rich Green

Title fonts courtesy of **Fontscafe.com**, © 2012
Photo of Amy Logan courtesy of **Moments By A**, MomentsByA.com

Published by
Full Heart Publishing
FullHeartPublishing.com

10 9 8 7 6 5 4 3 2 1

ISBN: 978-0-9890465-1-0

Printed in South Korea

GotYourCape.com
Facebook.com/AGirlWithACape

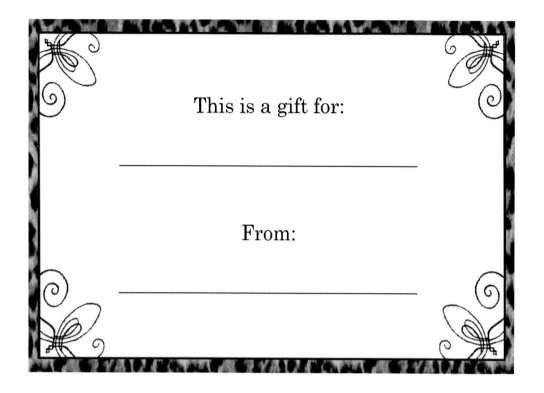

This is a gift for:

_____

From:

_____

This book is dedicated to my family and friends
for their incredible support and encouragement,
and all those who have helped me along the way.
Vince, Sadie & Scott, I love you very much.

And to all those who have ever felt, even for a second,
that they couldn't make a difference,
this book is for you.
Please don't ever forget—the world needs you.

xo,

amy

This is the story, it's so very true
of a girl with a cape, who's a lot like you.
She's smart, and she's kind, and she's funny as well.
I know you will like her, I can already tell!
You're smiling and waiting, "Just read it to me!"
Ok here we go ... on the count of three.

One.

Two.

Three.

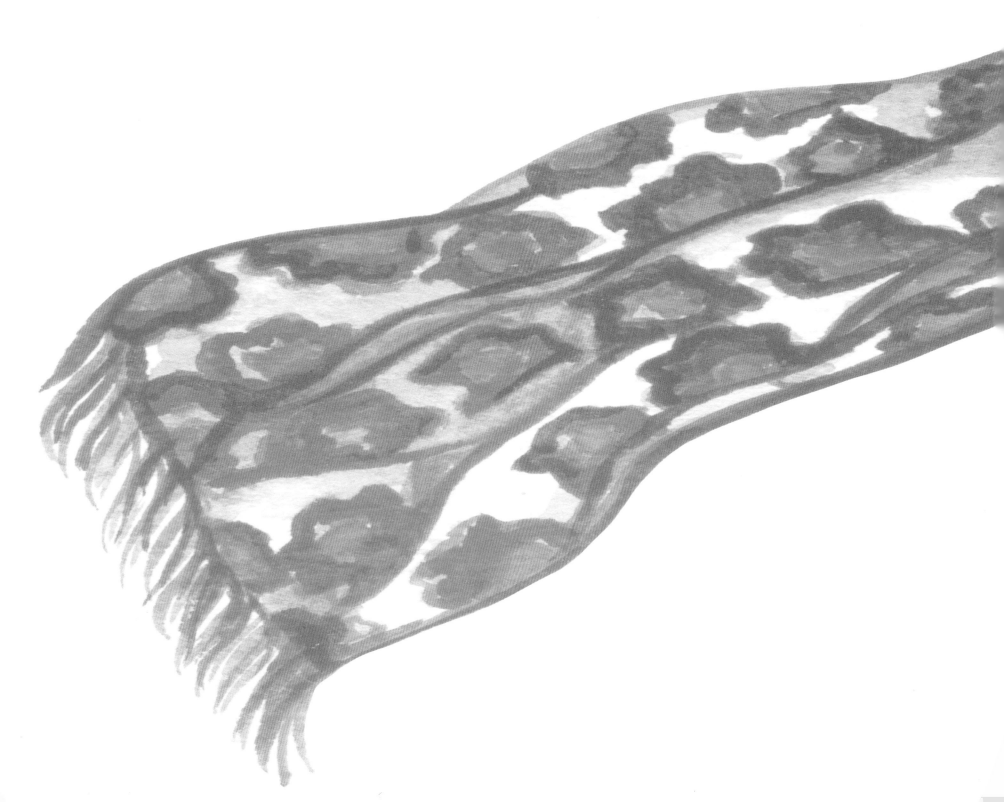

Once upon a time, there was a girl with a cape …

Well not so much a cape, but a scarf that she tied,
but it **FELT** like a cape because she felt **SUPER** inside.

The girl was so super, good came from her heart.
At night she couldn't wait for the next day to start!

So, after a quick night of super sweet dreams,
the morning sun rose with such light and bright beams.
The girl woke up Friday with such a big head.
She had this idea last night while in bed.

She now knew for certain that this would be great.
She hopped up at once and tied on her cape!

Like a superhero, this girl could do more,
which is why everyday, the scarf she wore.
It was her reminder to do such great things;
that when you do good, the *more* good it brings.

She ran down the stairs! *There's no time to brush teeth!*
(Ew gross! Back upstairs, brush the tops and underneath!)

She said to her mom, "Let's go to the store.
I have an idea of how I can do more.
You know all the pennies I have in my jar?
They're not doing much in the jar where they are.
So can we have breakfast then get in the car?
We don't even have to drive all that far."

Now what she was thinking, it's so very nice.
It's something that maybe you've heard once or twice,
that pennies are lucky when found on the ground...

and a girl with a cape was out on the town.

Want to know what she did with her pennies?

She and her mom
grabbed the jar.
They dropped a few
outside of their car.
They walked on the sidewalk,
dropped one or two.
They walked in the store,
where they dropped quite a few.
They added some pennies to the "help yourself" cup
then stood back in the distance and held their heads up.

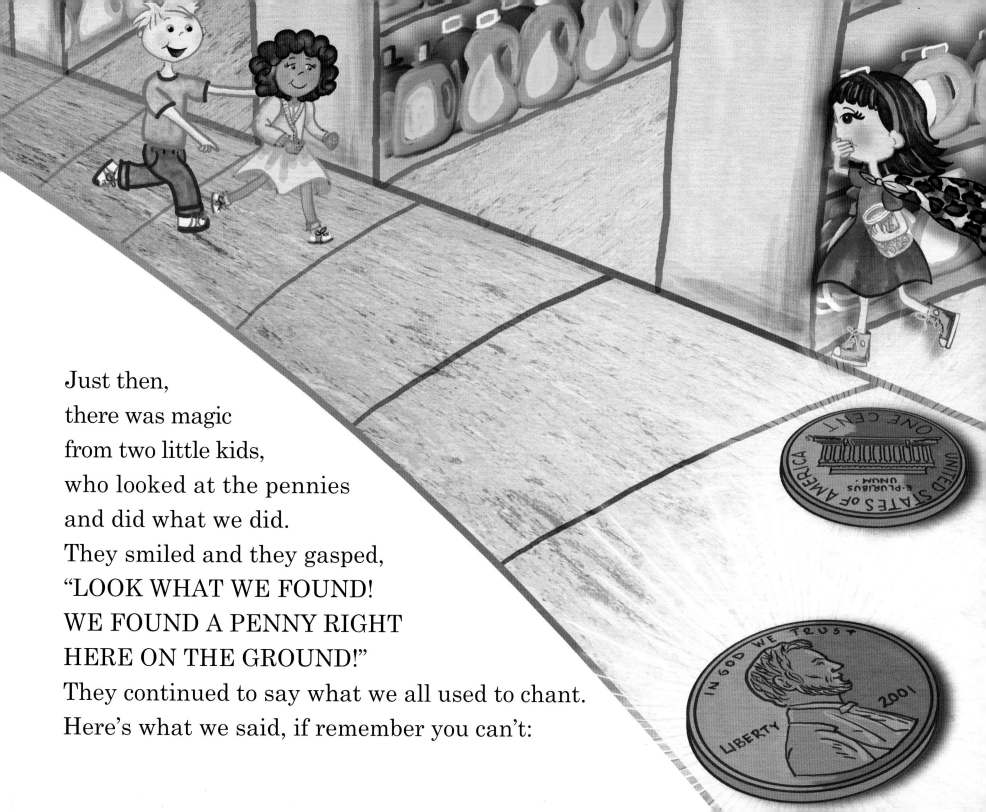

Just then,
there was magic
from two little kids,
who looked at the pennies
and did what we did.
They smiled and they gasped,
"LOOK WHAT WE FOUND!
WE FOUND A PENNY RIGHT
HERE ON THE GROUND!"
They continued to say what we all used to chant.
Here's what we said, if remember you can't:

"Find a penny, pick it up. All day long you'll have good luck."

Are you ready to see all the luck that they had?

The people who picked up the pennies that day,
their attitudes changed from what came their way:

A nice note from the neighbor, a good parking spot,
an 'A' on a test, ooh, she liked that a lot!
No line at the store, someone holding the door,
a shoe that stayed tied, oh my gosh and there's more!

A favorite snack, a free balloon,
a birthday card came extra soon.
A tooth fell out, tooth fairy came.
Dinner was great and dessert was the same!
Can you even stand all the luck that was found
from a couple of pennies found on the ground?

Whew!

She smiled so big, our girl with a cape.
She knew she did something so super great.
It made her feel good to make people feel good;
to do the nice things that all of us should.

But . . .

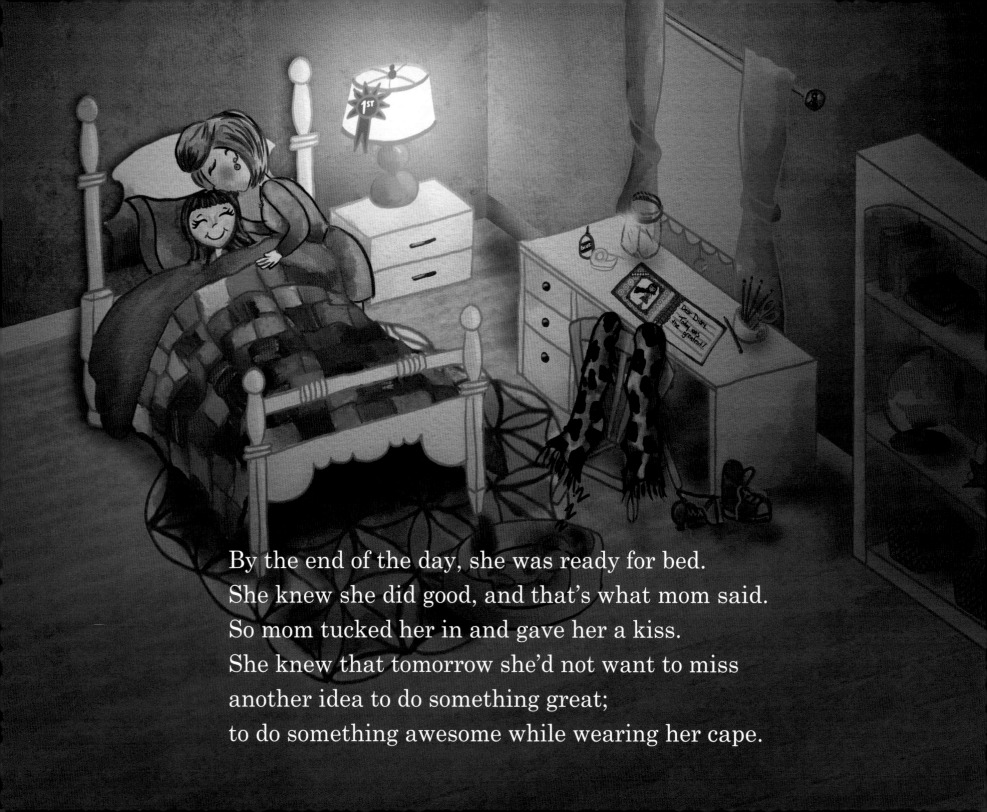

By the end of the day, she was ready for bed.
She knew she did good, and that's what mom said.
So mom tucked her in and gave her a kiss.
She knew that tomorrow she'd not want to miss
another idea to do something great;
to do something awesome while wearing her cape.

You see . . .

A girl with a cape, she knew this to be true:
the world is counting on us, what we do.
To make the world better, it starts here with you.
In case you don't know it, the world needs you too.

So pennies or nickels or some other thing,
it's just something kind the world needs you to bring.
You **ARE** a superhero, your powers are true.
The people around you are counting on you.

Time to get rest so tomorrow you too
can do something great …

So what next will *YOU* do?